ABC's for Boys

by Michael Kracht

MP

Majella Publishing

ABC's for Boys

First published in the United States of America in 2015 by
Majella Publishing LLC

First Edition

10 9 8 7 6

Library of Congress Control Number: 2015918270

ISBN: 978-0-692-56840-8

Printed and bound in China

All illustrations for this book were hand drawn in color pencil
by Michael Kracht through inspiration from his
children in heaven.

Hand drawn for my kids in heaven.

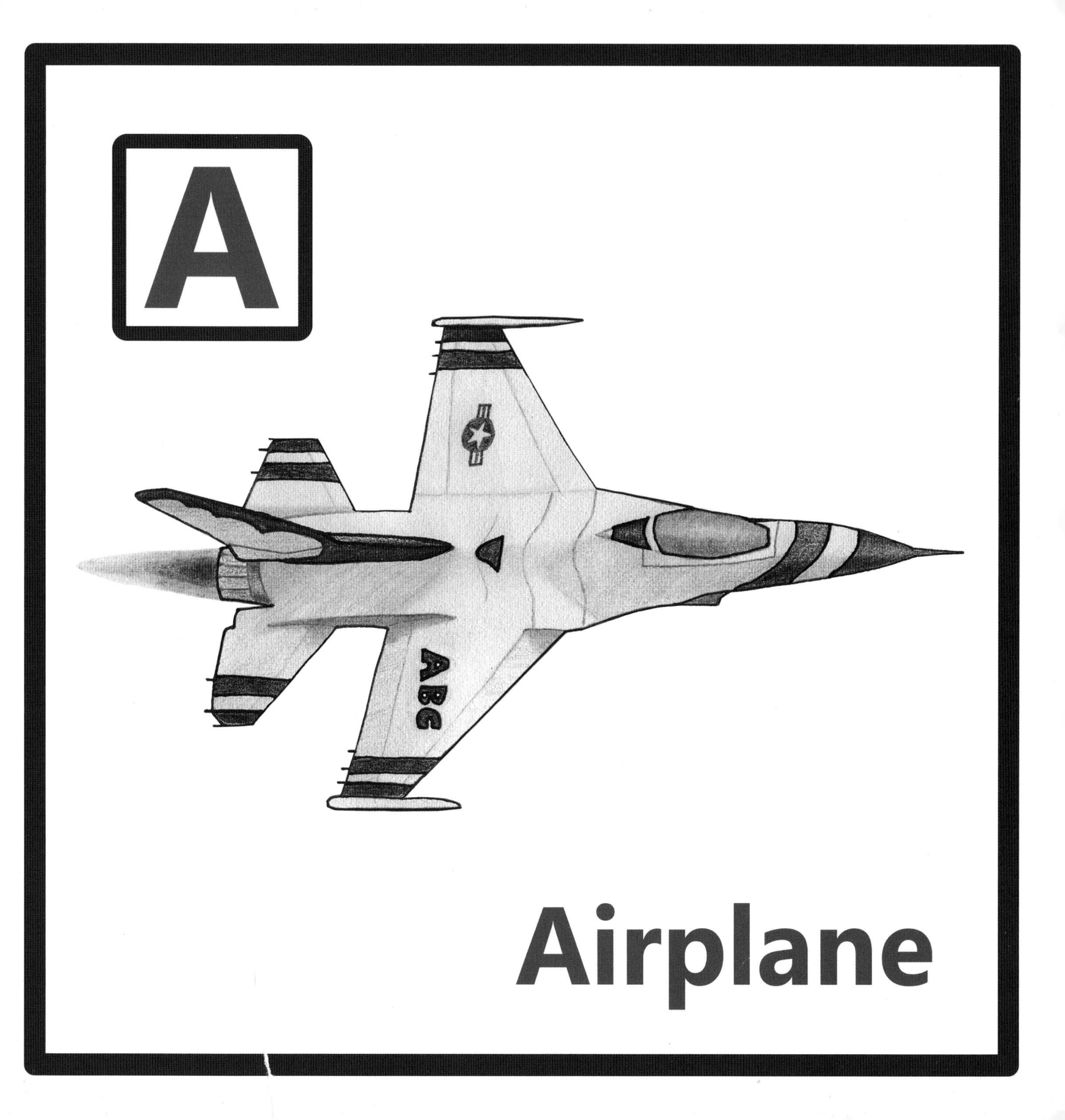
A
ABC
Airplane

B
Bulldozer

C
Car

D
Dog

E
Elephant

F
123
Firetruck

G
ABC
12
Garbage truck

H
ABC
123
Helicopter

I
Insect

J
Jack-o'-lantern

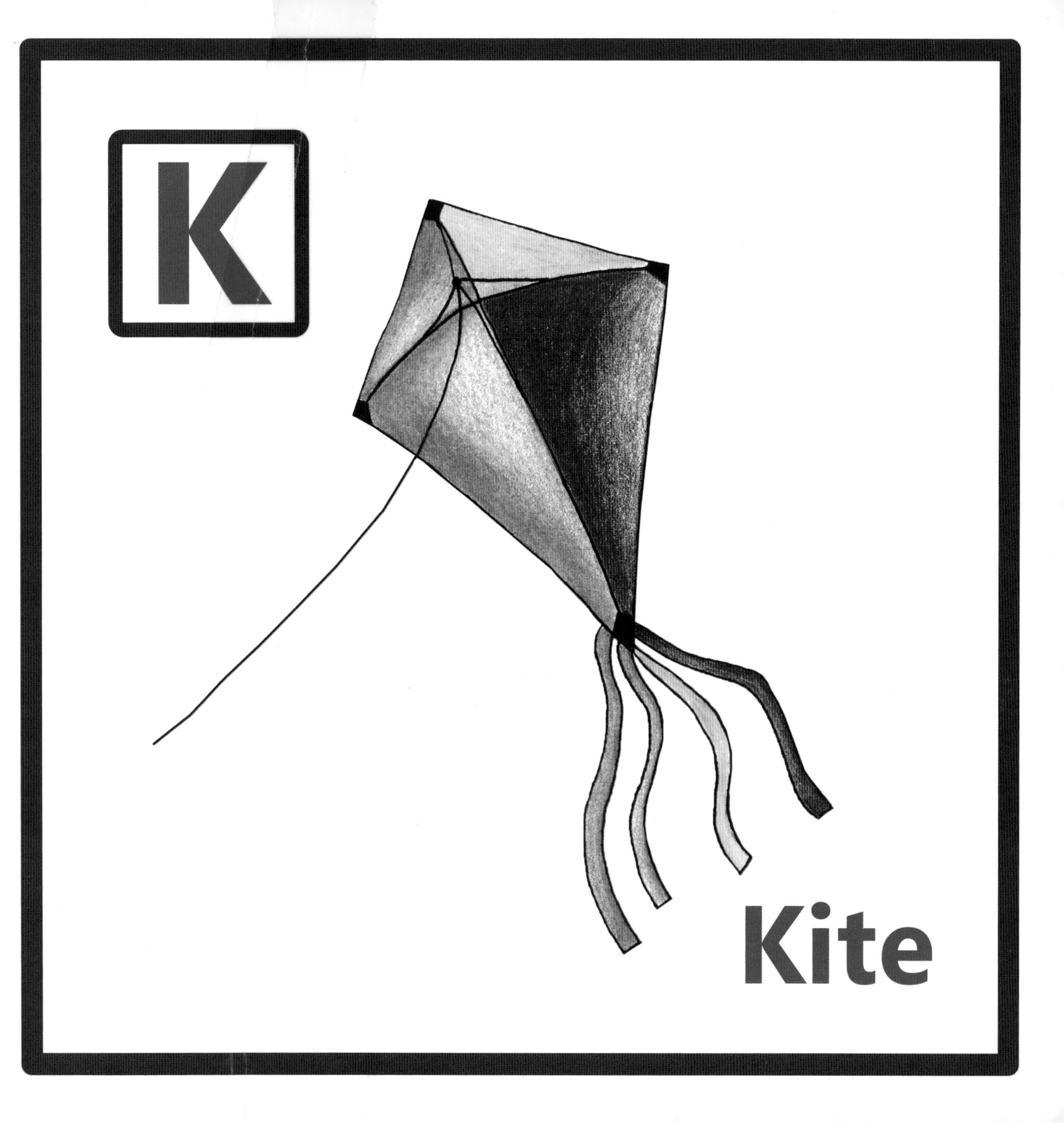
K
Kite

L
Lawn mower

M
ABC
Motorcycle

Numbers

O
Owl

P
ABC
Present

Q
ABC
25¢
1234
Quarter

R
Rocket

Sailboat

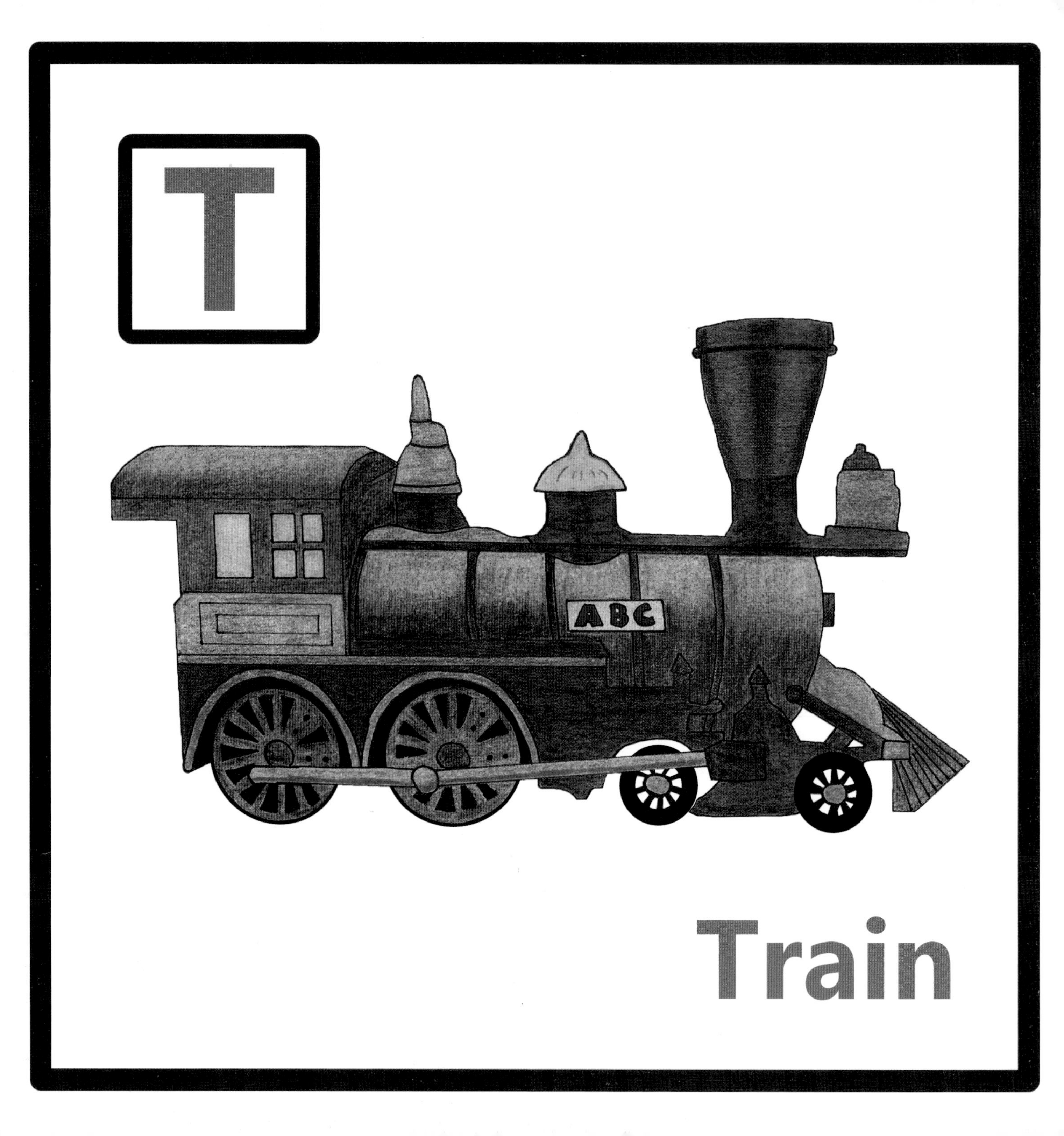
T
ABC
Train

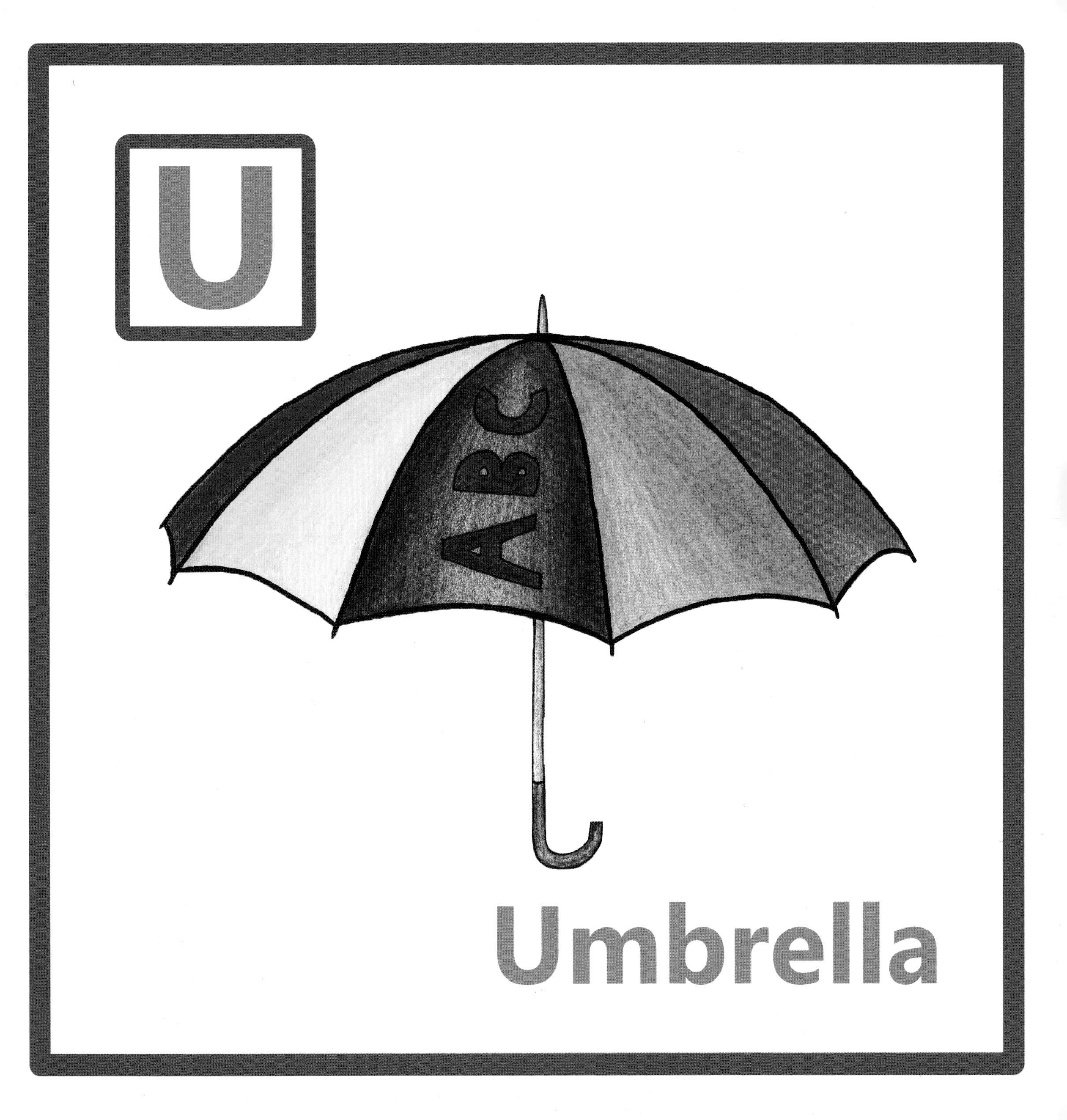
U
ABC
Umbrella

V
123
Vacuum

W
ABC
123
Wagon

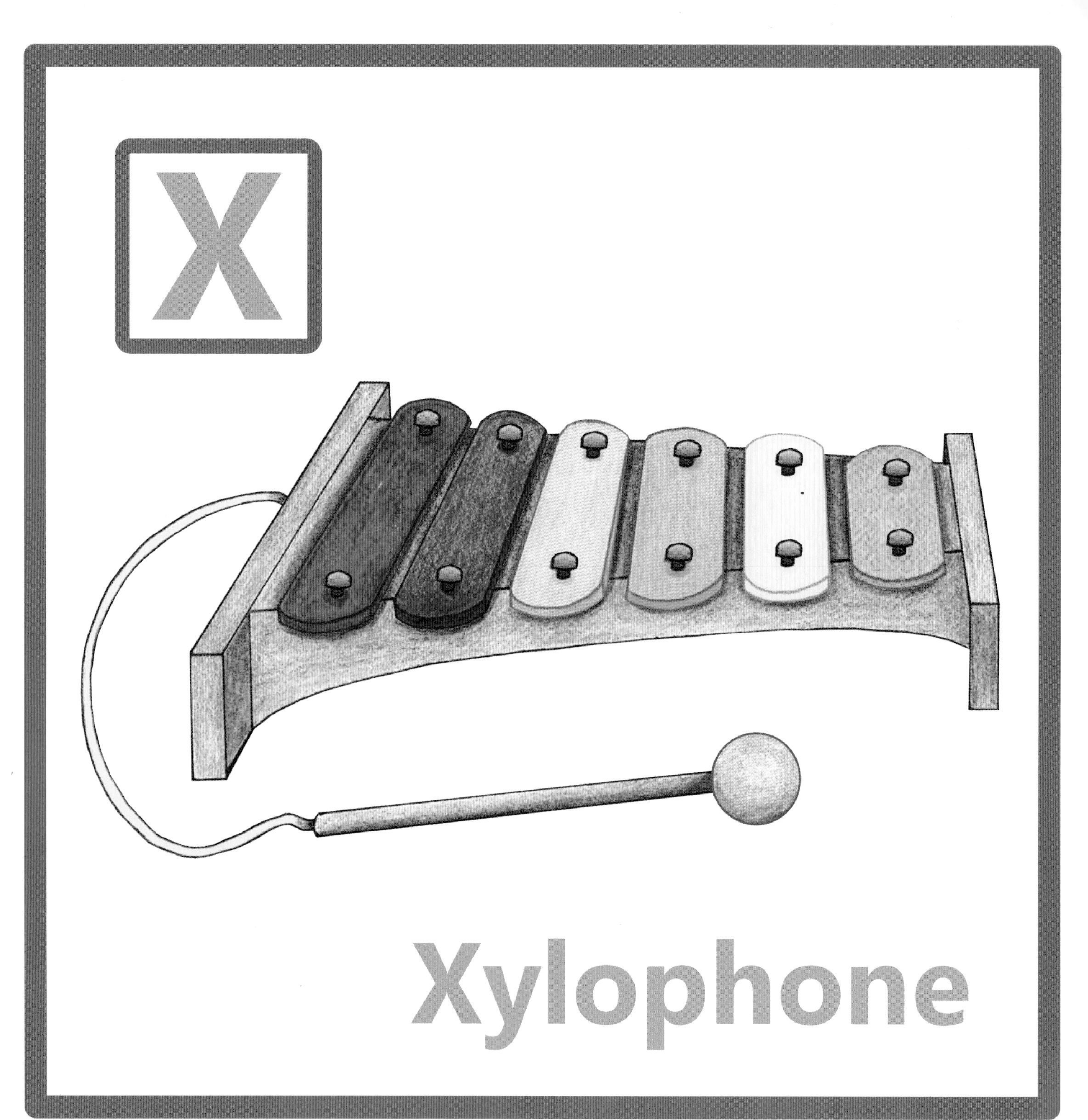
X
Xylophone

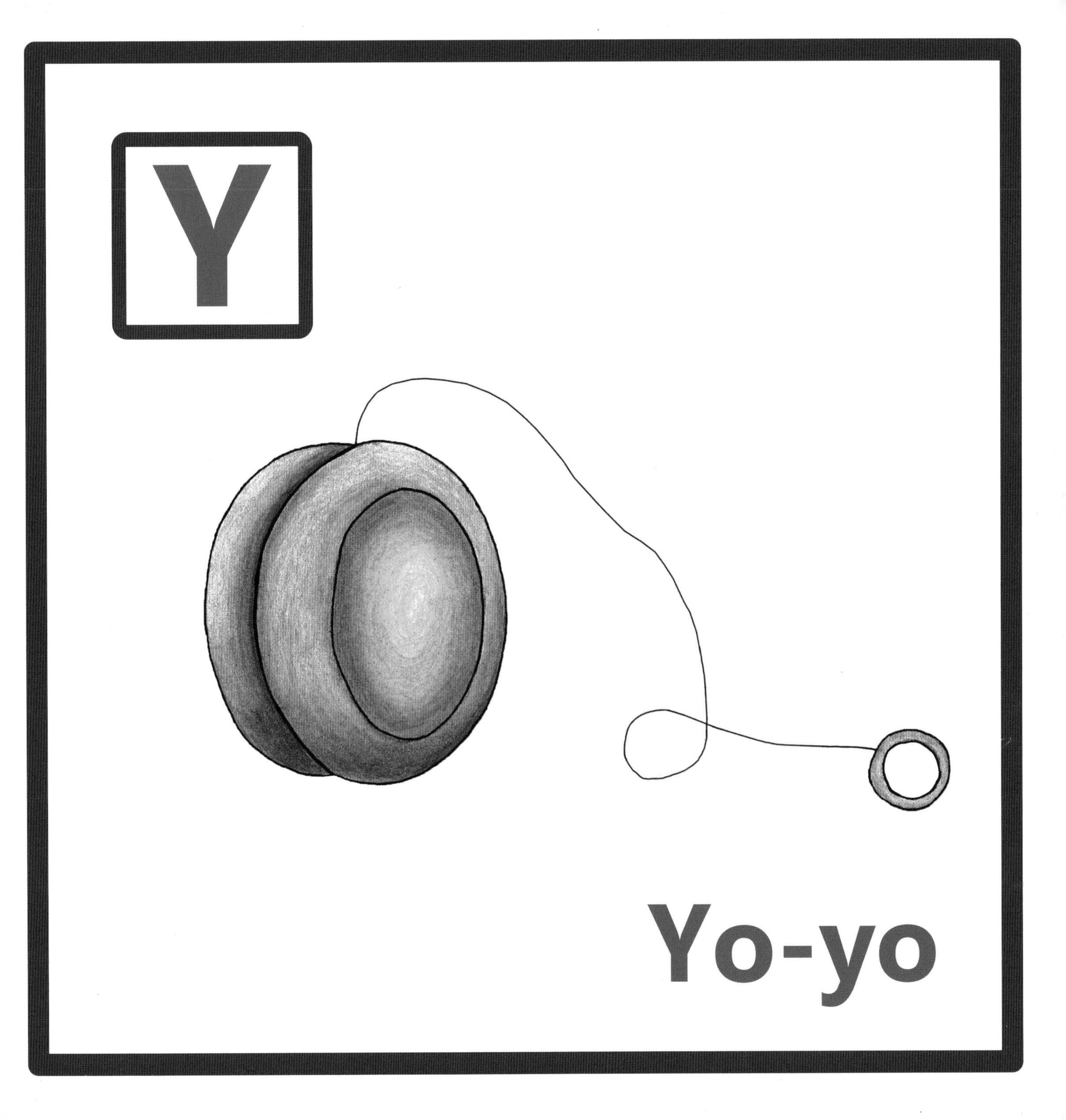
Y
Yo-yo

Z
ZOO
Zoo

A B C D E
F G H I J
K L M N O
P Q R S T
U V W X Y Z